5 Minute Bedtime Stories

5 Minute Bedtime Stories

tiger tales

Contents

GOOD NIGHT, LITTLE HARE

by Sheridan Cain
Illustrated by Sally Percy

GOOD NIGHT, SLEEP TIGHT!

by Claire Freedman
Illustrated by Rory Tyger

Can't You Sleep, Puppy?

★ ★

by Tim Warnes

10

Puppy couldn't sleep.
It was her first night
in her new home.

She tried sleeping
upside down.

She tried
snuggling up
to Penguin.

She even tried
lying on the floor.

AWOOOOOOOOOOOOO°

But still Puppy
couldn't sleep.

Puppy's howling woke up Pip the mouse.
"Can't you sleep, Puppy?" he asked.
"Perhaps you should try counting the stars
like I do."

But Puppy could
only count up to
one. *That* wasn't
enough to help
her to fall asleep.

What could she do next?

AWOOOOOOOOO

Susie the bird was awake now. "Can't you sleep, Puppy?" she twittered. "I always have a little drink before I go to bed."

Chirp!
Chirp!

Puppy went to her bowl
and had a little drink.

Slurp!
Slurp!

But then she made
a little puddle.
Well *that*
didn't help!
What *could* Puppy
do to get to sleep?

AWOOOOoooooo

Whiskers the rabbit had woken up, too.
"Can't you sleep, Puppy?" he mumbled
sleepily. "I hide away in my burrow
at bedtime. That always works."

Puppy dived under her blanket so that only her bottom was showing. But it was dark under there with no light at all.

Boing!

Puppy was too scared to go to sleep.

AWOOOOOOOOOOOO

25

Tommy the tortoise
poked his head out.

"Can't you sleep, Puppy?" he sighed. "I like to
sleep where it's bright and sunny."

Plod
Plod

Puppy liked that idea . . .

. . . and turned on her flashlight!

28

"Turn it off, Puppy!"
shouted all her friends.
"We can't get to sleep now!"

Poor Puppy was too tired to try
anything else.

Then Tommy had a great idea . . . .

He helped Puppy into her bed.
What Puppy needed for the
first night in her new home was . . .

. . . to snuggle up with *all* her new friends. Soon they were fast asleep. Good night, Puppy.

ZZZZZZZZZZ

33

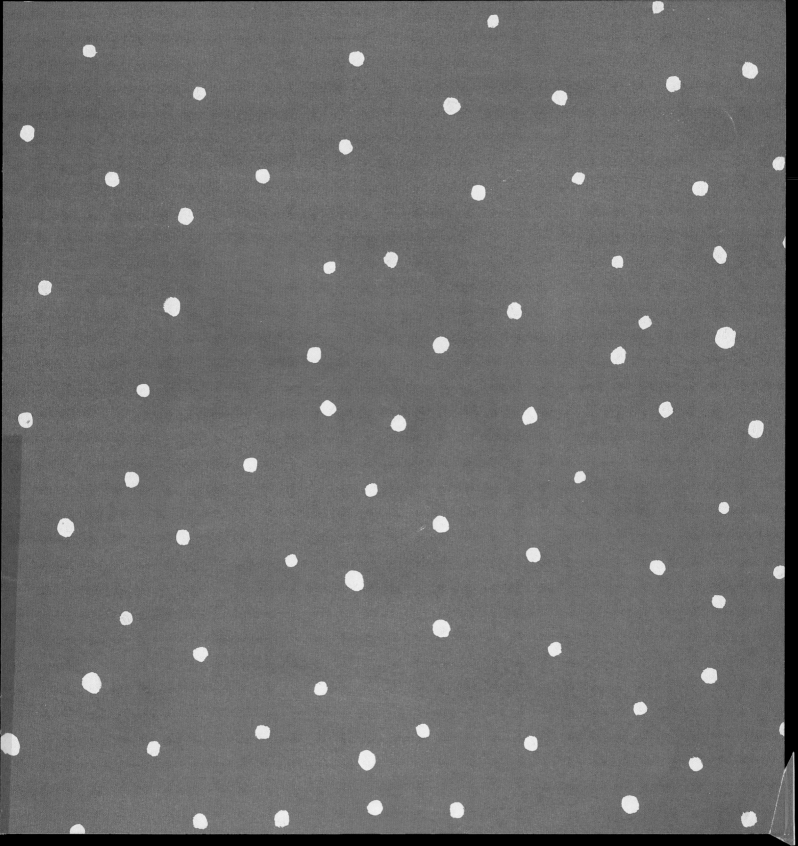

Night-Night, Newton

by Rory Tyger

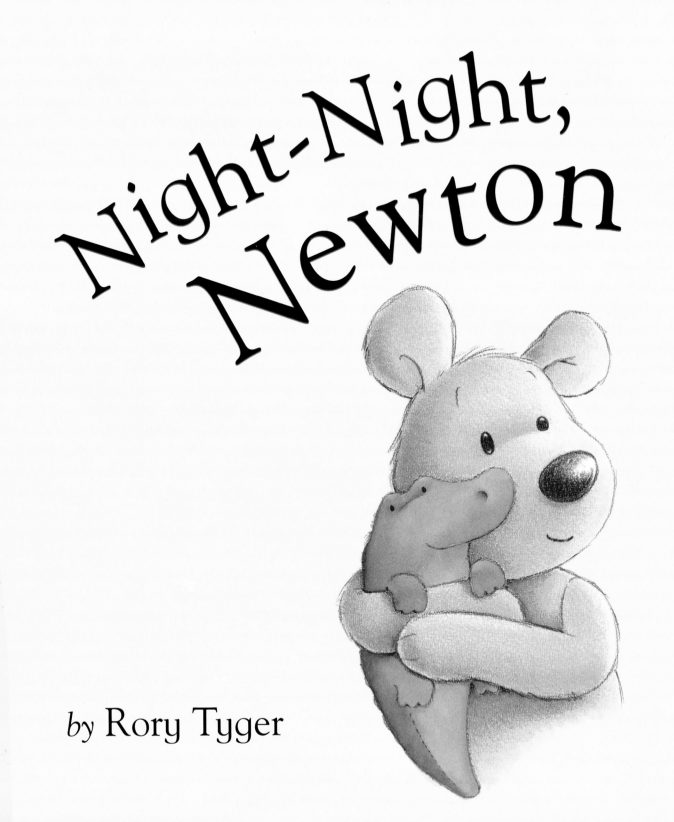

CREAK, CREAK, CRE-E-EAK!

Newton woke up suddenly. There was a funny noise somewhere in the room.

"Don't be scared," he told his toys. "There's always an explanation for everything."

He gave each of his toys a special cuddle so they wouldn't be scared.

CREAK, CREAK, CRE-E-EAK!

went the noise again.

Newton got out of bed and turned on the light.
He walked across the room . . . .

"See, toys," he said. "There's nothing to be scared of. It's only the closet door!"

Newton went back to bed again.

FLAP! FLAP! FLAP!

What was that? Was it a ghost?

Once more, Newton got out of bed. He wasn't really scared, but he took his bravest toy, Snappy, just in case. He tiptoed, very quietly, toward the noise.

FLAP! FLAP! FLAP!

"Of course!" said Newton . . .

"... just what I thought."
It was his bedroom curtains,
flapping in the breeze.
"I'll fix this," said Newton.

"You were very brave,
Snappy," he said, as
he closed the window.

SPLISH!

SPLASH!

SPLISH!

Another noise!

Newton looked outside. It wasn't raining.
Besides, the noise wasn't coming from outside.

It wasn't coming from his bedroom, either. What was it?

"Stay right there, you two," said Newton, "while I look around."

He wasn't the tiniest bit afraid. He was just taking Snappy with him for company.

Newton crept down the hallway. It was
very spooky, especially in the dark corners.

SPLISH! SPLASH! SPLISH!

went the noise.

Very, very quietly, Newton
opened the bathroom door . . . .

"Of course! We knew it was the bathroom
faucet, didn't we, Snappy?" said Newton.

Newton turned off the faucet and
tiptoed back down the hallway.
"Shh," he said to Snappy, just
in case something in the dark
corners sprang out at them.

Before he got into bed,
Newton pulled back the
curtains—just to check. It
was very, very quiet outside.

"No more funny noises,"
said Newton.

"You can go to sleep now,"
he told all of his toys.

RUMBLE! RUMBLE! RUMBLE!
"Oh, no!" cried Newton. "What's that?"

Newton listened very hard. Not a sound.
He was just beginning to think he hadn't
heard anything at all when . . .

RUMBLE! RUMBLE! RUMBLE!

There it was again!

Newton peered under his bed.
Nothing there at all—except for an old
piece of candy he'd forgotten about.
"Don't worry," Newton told his toys.
"We'll soon find out what it is."

RUMBLE!
Newton stood
very still.

RUMBLE!
Newton listened
very hard.

RUMBLE! went the noise.
And suddenly, Newton knew
exactly what it was!

Newton padded downstairs and into the kitchen.
He helped himself to a large glass of milk and two thick
slices of bread and honey. And now he couldn't hear a

RUMBLE! RUMBLE! RUMBLE!

at all, because . . .

. . . the rumbling had been
his empty tummy!

Newton went upstairs again and told his toys
about his rumbling tummy.

"There's always an explanation for everything,"
said Newton, as he climbed back into bed.
"Good night, everyone . . .

. . . sleep tight!"

SNORE, SNORE, SNORE!

went Newton.

What Are You Doing in My Bed?

by David Bedford
Illustrated by Daniel Howarth

Kip the kitten had nowhere to sleep
on a dark and cold winter's night.
So he crept through a door . . .

. . . and curled up warm and
snug in somebody's bed.
Then out of the dark,
Kip heard . . .

. . . whispers and hisses,
and soft feet padding
through the night.

Bright green eyes peered
in through the window,
and suddenly . . .

. . . one, two, three, four, five, six cats
came banging through the cat door!
They tumbled and skidded and rolled
across the floor, where they found . . .

73

. . . Kip!

"What are YOU doing in OUR bed?"
shouted the six angry cats.

"Your bed?" said Kip. "But this bed's too small for you. You'd never all fit!"

"Never fit?" said the cats. "Just you watch . . . ."

One, two, three cats curled up
neatly, head to tail . . .
then four, five, six cats
piled on top.

"See? There's no room for you," they said. "You'd never fit." "Never fit?" said Kip. "Just you watch . . . ."

Tottering and teetering, Kip carefully climbed
on top. "I'll sleep here," he said.
   "Okay," the cats yawned.
"But don't fidget or snore."
And they fell asleep in a heap.
   But suddenly, a big, deep,
growly voice said . . .

"WHAT ARE YOU DOING IN MY BED? SCRAM!"

The cats scattered around the room, but they only found hard, cold places to sleep.

Harry the dog was comfy in his bed,
and he soon began to snore.
But then an icy wind whistled in
through the cat door, and Harry
awoke and shivered.

Kip whispered, "Follow me," and
he quickly led six cold cats
across the floor . . .

. . . to the cozy bed.
"We'll keep you warm,"
said Kip.

"You'll never all fit," chattered Harry.
"Never fit?" said Kip. "Just you watch . . . ."

Kip and Harry snored right through the night under their warm blanket of cats.

And they all fit purr-fectly!

Bedtime, Little Ones!

by Claire Freedman ★ *Illustrated by* Gail Yerrill

It's been such a happy day playing;
The setting sun glows golden red.
The little ones run home for supper,
For soon it will be time for bed.

Mommy Mouse smiles
at her children,
"Time for bed,
when you've
finished your teas!"
"We're not at all tired!"
the mice chorus,
But someone's asleep
in her cheese!

It's bathtime—five rabbits are splashing,
Having fun in their big bubbly tub!
"We love to splish-splosh!" they tell Mommy,
As she gives each small bunny a scrub.

Mommy Rabbit is
drying her bunnies,
And counting them,
"One, two, three, four . . . ."

Then she giggles,
"Wait—somebody's missing!
There should be just
one bunny more!"

The little ones snuggle 'round Grandpa,
As he reads to them tales from his book.
"And another!" cries one little badger.
"There's a great story here,
Grandpa—look!"

Mommy Squirrel says,
"Bedtime, my babies,
Hear the sleepy-train
calling choo-choo!"
But one little squirrel's
not sleepy;
She still wants to
play peekaboo!

The little bears gaze at the night sky,
As bright silver stars start to peep.
"One, two, three, ZZZZ!" snores the youngest.
Star-counting has sent him to sleep!

Little Rabbit is searching all over.
"Oh, no!" he cries. "Where's Little Ted?
I must find my cuddly bear, Mommy;
I can't sleep without him in bed!"

All the animals have their own teddies
To cuddle and snuggle up tight.
With each of their soft toys beside them,
They're sure to sleep soundly all night!

As Mommy Mouse
tucks in each baby,
She whispers, "Good night,
sleepyhead!"
Then Little Mouse
copies her Mommy,
And she tucks in her
own toy in bed.

The hedgehogs are drifting to sleep now,
As Daddy sings sweet lullabies.
But one little hedgehog is singing along—
"Tra-la-la! I love Daddy!" he cries.

111

Good night,
little badgers
and squirrels,
Sleep tight, little
bears and mice, too;
Sweet dreams,
little hedgehogs
and rabbits,
And night-night
and sweet dreams
to YOU!

Bedtime
for Little Bears!

by David Bedford   Illustrated by Caroline Pedler

Little Bear and his mother
had spent a long, sunny day
exploring in the snow.

"It's getting late," said Mother Bear. "It will soon be bedtime. Let's go home, Little Bear."

Little Bear flopped down in the snow and wiggled his tail. "I'm not sleepy," he said.

Mother Bear smiled. "Would you like to take one more walk," she said, "and see who else is going to bed?"

Little Bear looked around. "Who else *is* going to bed?" he wondered.

Mother Bear stretched up tall to find out.

"Look over there," she said.

"It's Little Owl!" said Little Bear.

"Little Owl likes to stretch her wings before bedtime, and feel the whisper of the soft night breeze in her feathers," said Mother Bear.

Little Bear scrambled onto his mother's shoulders.

"I like flying, too!" he said.

As Mother Bear climbed to the top of a hill, Little Bear felt the wind whispering and tickling through his fur.

Then he saw someone else . . . .

"Who's that?" said Little Bear, giggling. "And what's he doing?"

"Baby Hare is having a bath in the snow," said Mother Bear, "so that he's clean and drowsy, and ready for sleep."

"I like snow baths, too," said Little Bear. He dove into the snow and plopped a big, soft snowball on Mother Bear's nose.

Little Bear and his mother
laughed as they flopped
down together in a heap.

"Are you sleepy now, Little
Bear?" his mother asked as
they lay together in the snow,
watching the first bright stars
twinkling in the sky.

Little Bear blinked his tired eyes as he tried not to yawn. "I want to see who else is going to bed," he said.

"We'll have to be quiet now," said Mother Bear. "Some little ones will already be asleep."

"Look over there," whispered Mother Bear. "Little Fox likes being cuddled and snuggled to sleep by his mother."

Little Bear pressed close against Mother Bear's warm fur. "I like cuddles, too," he said.

"We'll be home soon," said his mother softly.

But Little Bear had just seen somebody else . . . .

"I can see whales!" he said, turning to look out across the starlit sea.

"Little Whale likes his mother to sing him softly to sleep," said Mother Bear.

Little Bear sat with his mother and watched the whales swimming by until they were gone, leaving only the soothing hum of their faraway song.

Then Little Bear climbed onto his mother's back. As he was carried home, he watched the colors that flickered and brushed across the sky, while his mother sang him a lullaby.

"I like songs, too," he told his mother.

"And now," said Mother Bear very softly, "it's time for little bears to go to sleep."

Little Bear nestled into his mother's soft fur, and when she gave him a gentle kiss good night . . .

139

. . . Little Bear was
already fast asleep.

Under the Silvery Moon

by Colleen McKeown

The stars were shining brightly.
Little Kitten was in bed.
But up he sat, still wide awake;
"Sleep now," his mother said.

"But it's so noisy, I can't sleep!"
said Kitten with a cry.
"It's just our friends," said Mother Cat.
"They're waking up nearby . . . .

The tiny mice are playing;
    they explore the barn at night.
They skip and scamper here and there
    beneath the warm lamplight.

Hush, Kitten; can you hear it—
that shuffling, snuffling sound?
The hedgehogs look for food to eat
along the moonlit ground.

That cry you hear, so long and loud,
that distant, haunting tune,
Belongs to Fox, who's up at night.
He's calling to the moon.

Around us swirls a summer song;
   it's whispered through the trees.
The evening wind is blowing
   through the softly rustling leaves.

Beyond the midnight meadow,
    where the air is soft and cool,
The frogs are gently croaking
    all around the moonlit pool.

Some creatures are not stirring;
they do not make a peep.
Like us, they've had a busy day,
and now they're fast asleep.

The badgers stretch their sturdy legs
and blink into the dark.
'It's bedtime,' they are calling,
with a deep and playful bark.

The nimble hares are dancing;
their paws thump on the ground.
With joyful leaps they chase their tails
and spring and dart around.

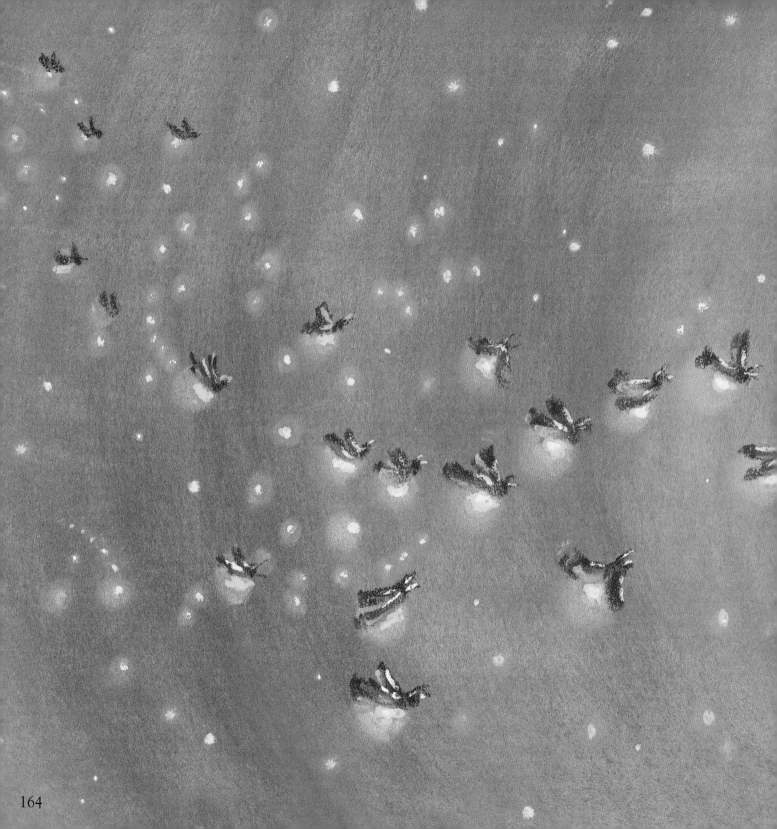

Something quiet and gentle
 lights up the dark night skies.
Glowing warm and lovely
 are the dreamy fireflies.

Owl is hooting softly;
across the stars she glides.
Soaring home toward the barn,
upon the wind she rides.

And so you see, my little one,
  there's nothing you should fear.
Our friends' nighttime adventures
  are all that you can hear."

Little Kitten closed his eyes
  and hugged his mother tight.
"It's time you went to sleep," she purred.
  "Sweet dreams, my love; good night."

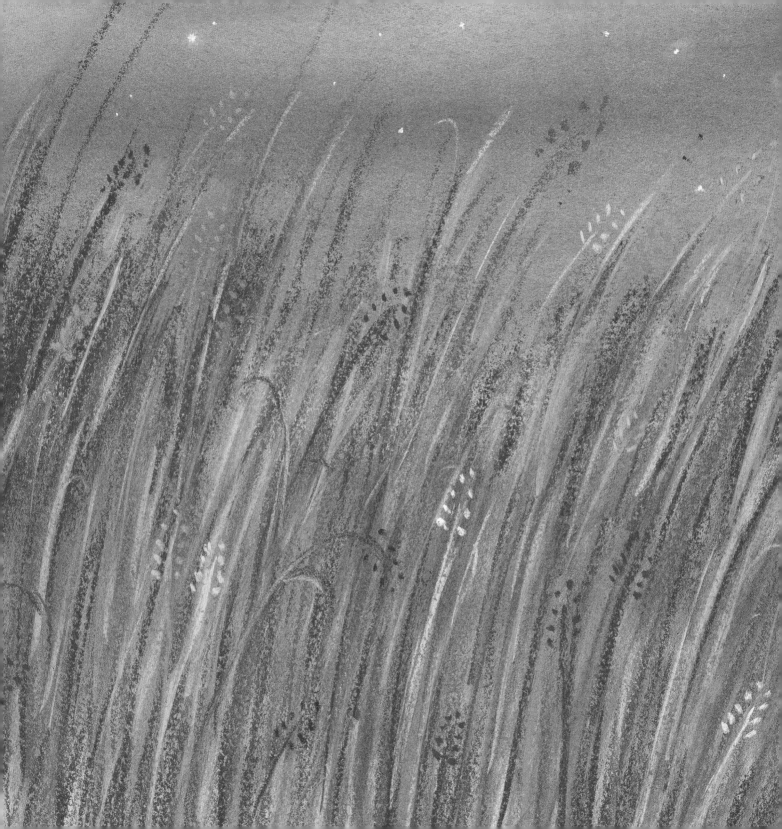

Time to Sleep, Little Bear!

by Catherine Walters

"It's nearly bedtime, Little Bear,"
called Mother Bear, gathering
up his baby brother and sister.
"Come along—time for your bath."

Little Bear sat by the edge of the lake.

The fish leaped to catch the evening flies.

Huh! The fish aren't going to bed, thought
Little Bear. *Why should I?*

It gave him an idea . . . .

"Look! I'm a fish!" shouted Little Bear. "I don't have to go to bed!"

He began to jump and dive and splash.

"Don't do that," sighed Mother Bear.

"The babies are getting too excited to sleep."

When they had all calmed down,
Mother Bear took them back home.
"Go and get some nice, cool grass
for bedding, Little Bear," she said.
"That will help you sleep."

Little Bear went outside and pulled up
a few pawfuls of grass.

Some owls were swooping through
the meadow.

The owls aren't going to bed, thought
Little Bear. *Why should I?*

Little Bear rushed back into the cave and began to flap his arms. "Look! I'm an owl!" he hooted. "I don't need to go to bed."

"Oh, Little Bear, stop that!" groaned Mother Bear. "Look, the babies are throwing all their comfy bedding around, too. None of you will have anywhere to sleep."

186

At last, Little Bear and the babies were safely in bed.
"I think you need a nice, gentle song," said
Mother Bear. "Now, close your eyes."
Little Bear wasn't listening. Outside, he could
hear wolves howling.
The wolves aren't going to sleep,
he thought. *Why should I?*

"Look, I'm a wolf! AAAAOOOW!" said Little Bear.

"OW, OW, OW!" shrieked the babies.

"That's enough, Little Bear," Mother Bear growled.

"I don't want any little wolves in the cave. You can wait outside until the babies are asleep."

"Hooray!" cried Little Bear, running outside.
He charged across the meadow howling,
"AAAAOOOW!"
Then, from somewhere close by,
someone answered him, "AAAAOOOW!"

Little Bear jumped. There in front of him was
a wolf cub, with his family close by.

"Are you a wolf?" the cub asked. "You
sound like one, but you don't look like one."

"Are you sure you're a wolf?" called
a big, gruff voice . . . .

". . . because you look like a little bear to me!"

"I'm a bear, I'm a bear!" shouted Little Bear, as Father Bear picked him up.

"Good night, Little Bear," called the wolf cubs.

Father Bear snuggled Little Bear into his fur.

"So you're a bear?" he said. "But are you
a sleepy bear all ready for bed?"

"No," said Little Bear. "I'm not—"

But before he could finish speaking,
he had fallen fast asleep.

Hush-a-bye Lily

by Claire Freedman

Illustrated by John Bendall-Brunello

Nighttime crept over the barnyard. But Lily pricked up her ears. "What's that quacking sound?" she asked.

"Hush now!" said Mother Rabbit. "It's only the ducks, resting in the tall reeds."

203

"Sorry, Lily!" Duck called out. "Are we keeping you awake? We were singing sleepy bedtime songs.

"Would you like me to sing you a song, too?"

"Yes, please!" Lily said.

So Duck puffed out his chest, shook out his feathers,
and sang the most beautiful duck lullaby he knew.
"That was lovely!" sighed Lily.
And without a sound, Duck waddled away,
back to the moonlit pond.

"Hoo-hoo, hoo-hoo!"
hooted Owl.
  "Hush!" whispered
Lily's mother.

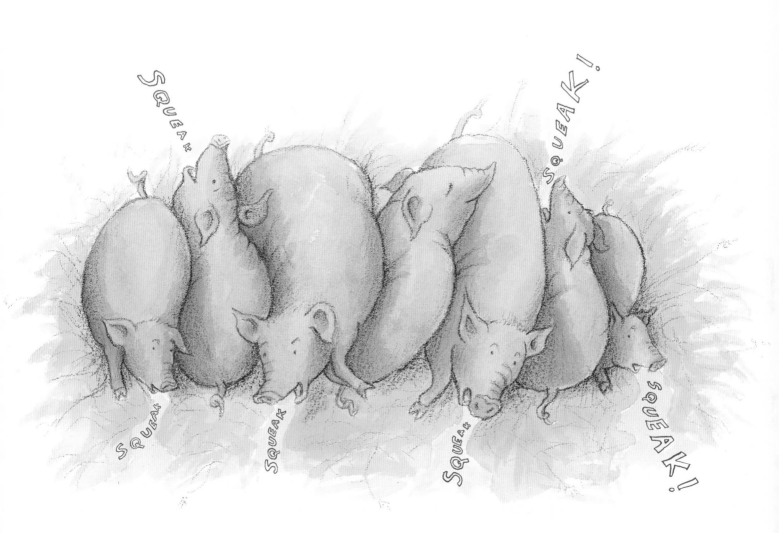

"Squeak, squeak," yawned the piglets.

"Shhh!" sighed Mother Rabbit. "Hush!"

Then Lily pricked up her ears again. "What's that mooing sound?" she asked.

"Hush now!" said Mother Rabbit. "It's only the cows lowing in the cowshed."

"Sorry, Lily!" said Cow. "We were just telling each other bedtime stories. Would you like to hear a story, too?"

"Yes, please!" said Lily.

So Cow told Lily her favorite sleepy bedtime tale.
"That was nice!" Lily yawned.
Cow lumbered back to the barn,
as quietly as she could.

"Meow!" cried Cat,
   huddling her kittens together.

"Hee-haw!" brayed Donkey,
turning in his sleep.
"Shhh!" sighed Lily's mother.
"Hush now!"

Then Lily pricked up her ears once more.

"What's that clucking sound?" she asked.

"It's only the hens hiding in the haystacks," said Mother Rabbit.

"Sorry, Lily!" called out Hen. "We were collecting straw for our beds. Would you like some, too?"

"Oooh, yes!" said Lily.

So Hen brought back a beakful of
straw and tucked it under Lily's head.
"That's cozy," said Lily, sleepily.
Then Hen crept off softly to the
hen coop, on tiptoes.

"Shhh!" hushed the ducks
to the rippling reeds.

"Shhh!" hushed the cows
to the leaves on the trees.

"Shhh!" hushed the hens
to the whispering wind.

Ssshhhh

"Hush now, Lily!" whispered Mother Rabbit,
and she snuggled up against her little one.
The moon hid behind the clouds.
All was quiet and still, until . . .

. . . down in the stable,

Little Foal pricked up his ears.

"What's that whistling sound?" he asked.

"Shhh, go back to sleep!" his mother whispered.

"It's only little Lily snoring!"

Good Night, Little Hare

by Sheridan Cain

Illustrated by Sally Percy

Under the silvery moon, Little Hare
lay with eyes tightly shut. For his
blanket he had the sky, and the soft
hay formed his bed.

"Good night, Little Hare," Mother Hare
whispered.

231

Just then, Mole came by. "You cannot leave your baby there," he said. "The farmer cuts the hay at dawn."

"But what can I do?" asked Mother Hare. "Where can Little Hare sleep?"

"You should dig a hole!" said Mole.

So Mother Hare began to dig.

She scraped and scraped
at the soft, brown earth, until
the hole was big and deep. Then
she carried Little Hare to his new bed.

But Little Hare did not like it. "Mama," he cried. "It's so dark and I cannot sleep."

"Mother Hare," said Badger, who was bumbling along, "you cannot leave your baby in the dark."

"But where can Little Hare sleep?"
asked Mother Hare.
"You should cover him in a
bed of leaves," said Badger.

So Mother Hare hurried
and she scurried.

She made a soft, round pile with
the leaves. Then she carried Little
Hare to his new bed.

But Little Hare did not like it.

"Mama," he cried. "I don't like the crinkly-crackly noise my new bed makes."

239

Blackbird heard Little Hare's cry from his tree.

"Mother Hare," he said, "you cannot leave your baby there."

"But where can Little Hare sleep?" asked Mother Hare.

"What you need is a nest up high," said Blackbird.

So Mother Hare placed
Little Hare in an empty
bird's nest.

But Little Hare did not like it.
"Mama," he cried, looking down,
"it's high up here and I might
fall out."

So Mother Hare carried Little Hare down again. She did not know what to do. "Oh, dear," she sighed. "How can I find the right bed for Little Hare?"

Owl was watching
from his perch.

"Don't you remember how your mother kept you safe when *you* were young?" he said.

Mother Hare remembered how the sky had been her blanket and the soft, golden hay had been her bed.

She remembered how, from dusk to dawn, her mother had watched over her.

The sun was just rising.
Mother Hare's eyes
became bright. The
farmer had come early,
and the hay was cut.

It was quite safe
there now.

Mother Hare carried Little Hare back to
his old bed and lay him gently down.

"Mama," said Little Hare.
"This is my own bed, and I
like it."

Then everyone whispered,
"Good night, Little Hare!"

Good Night, Sleep Tight!

by Claire Freedman
Illustrated by Rory Tyger

One night, Ethan just could not fall asleep.

"Aren't you sleepy, Ethan?" asked Mommy.

"No," replied Ethan. "I don't feel sleepy at all. I'm wide awake!"

"Do you have your favorite friends to cuddle up with?" she asked. "They might help you fall asleep."

259

"I have Tiger and Rabbit,"
said Ethan. "But where's
Elephant?"

"Here he is," said Mommy,
tucking him in nice and snug.
"Now you'll feel sleepy."

But neither Ethan nor his
little friends went to sleep.
"We're still wide awake,
Mommy," he said.

"What about a cup of nice
warm milk?" said Mommy.
"That makes me
sleepy."

Ethan drank every drop of his warm milk. But he didn't feel sleepy.

"I'm still wide awake, Mommy," he said. "Can we watch the fireflies? They might make me sleepy."

Mommy wrapped Ethan in his cozy blanket, and together they watched the dancing fireflies. Ethan tried to count them, but they didn't make him feel sleepy.

"I'm still wide awake, Mommy," he said. "Would you sing me a lullaby, please? That might make me tired."

Mommy sang some of
Ethan's favorite songs.
Ethan closed his eyes and listened
. . . but he didn't feel sleepy.
"I'm still wide awake," he whispered.
"I know, Ethan," Mommy said.
"Let me rock you in my arms. That
will make you sleepy."

Mommy rocked Ethan gently in
her arms, all the way down to
the apple orchard and back.
Ethan felt safe and warm,
but he didn't feel the
tiniest bit sleepy.

"Mommy, I'm STILL wide awake!" he said. "Will you tell me a story, please? Listening to stories makes me feel sleepy."

Mommy settled Ethan on her lap,
and he snuggled up close.

She told him stories
about all the funny
things she had done
when she was little
—just like him.

"Sometimes I didn't
feel sleepy
at bedtime either,"
Mommy said.

Mommy carried Ethan back inside.
She smiled a secret smile as she
remembered how her mommy
used to put her to bed
when she was little.

Mommy tucked Ethan into bed. She pulled the covers right up to his nose.

"My mommy used to tuck me into bed with the blankets pulled right up to my nose—like this!" she said.

"Then she'd
stroke the
top of my head—
like this,"
Mommy said.
  Very gently, she
stroked the top of Ethan's head.

"And she'd give me a special kiss
good night," said Mommy.
She gave Ethan a very
special kiss good night.

"What next, Mommy?" said Ethan, with a big yawn.
"And then she'd say, 'Good night, sleep tight!'"
said Mommy.

"Good night, Mommy," yawned Ethan . . . .

But before Mommy could say, "Sleep tight," Ethan was fast asleep!

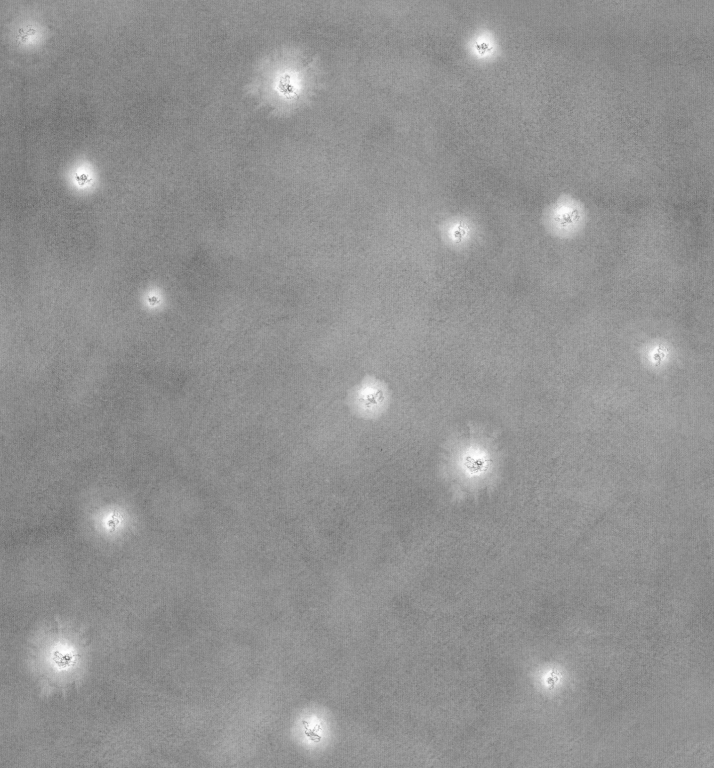

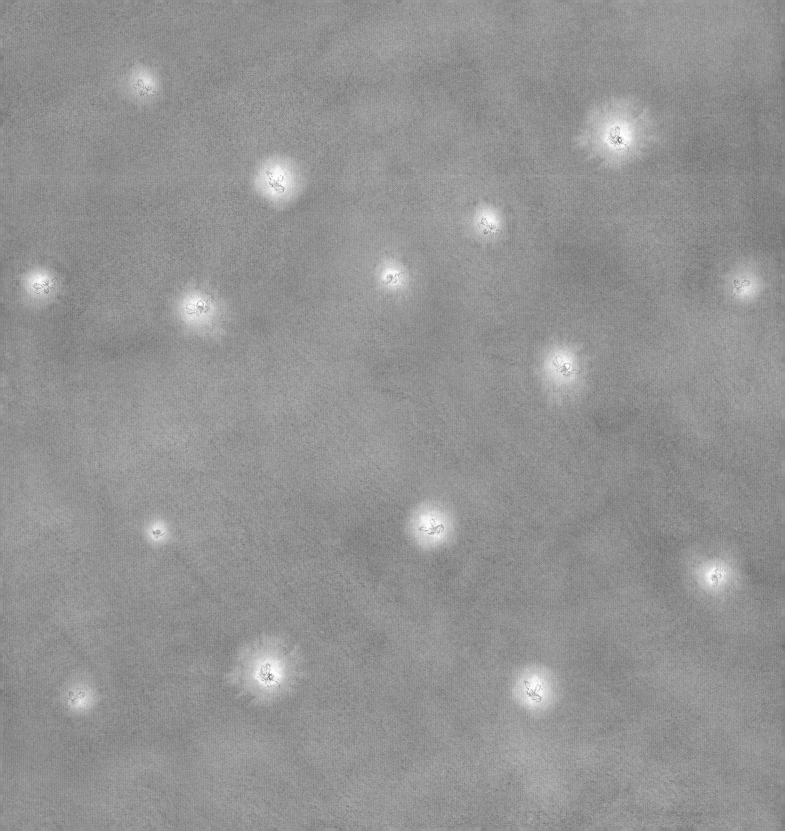

5 MINUTE BEDTIME STORIES

tiger tales

5 River Road, Suite 128, Wilton, CT 06897
Published in the United States 2014
Originally published in Great Britain 2012
by Little Tiger Press

LTP/1800/1198/0415
ISBN 13: 978-1-58925-507-4
ISBN 10: 1-58925-507-0
Printed in China

For more insight and activities,
visit us at www.tigertalesbooks.com

GOOD NIGHT, LITTLE HARE

by Sheridan Cain
Illustrated by Sally Percy

First published in Great Britain 1999
by Little Tiger Press

GOOD NIGHT, SLEEP TIGHT!

by Claire Freedman
Illustrated by Rory Tyger

First published in Great Britain 2003
by Little Tiger Press